First American Edition 1996 by Kane/Miller Book Publishers
Brooklyn, New York & La Jolla, California

Originally published in Great Britain in 1996 by Andersen Press Ltd.
Text copyright © 1996 by Sarah Garland.
Illustrations copyright © 1996 by Tony Ross.

Library of Congress Catalog Card Number 95-82006
ISBN 0-916291-64-2

Printed and bound in Italy by Grafiche AZ, Verona
1 2 3 4 5 6 7 8 9 10

# Sarah Garland • Tony Ross

## Seeing Red

A CRANKY NELL BOOK

KM Kane/Miller Book Publishers

Brooklyn, New York & La Jolla, California

TREWENNA'S DAD was a fisherman. Trewenna's gran stayed at home and minded Trewenna. Every day Gran baked the pasties, and put the soup to boil, and knitted warm, red, woollen, itchy socks for Trewenna, and sewed warm, red flannel, scratchy petticoats for Trewenna. And every day she made Trewenna put them on before she was allowed to run outside, down to the beach to gut the fish, or up on the cliffs to keep the crows from the barley.

"You never can tell when that scoundrel Napoleon might come sailing up the coast with his French warships," said her gran. "You must always be prepared with good, warm clothing."

But as soon as Trewenna was round the corner, she always took off her socks and petticoat and hid them under a stone.

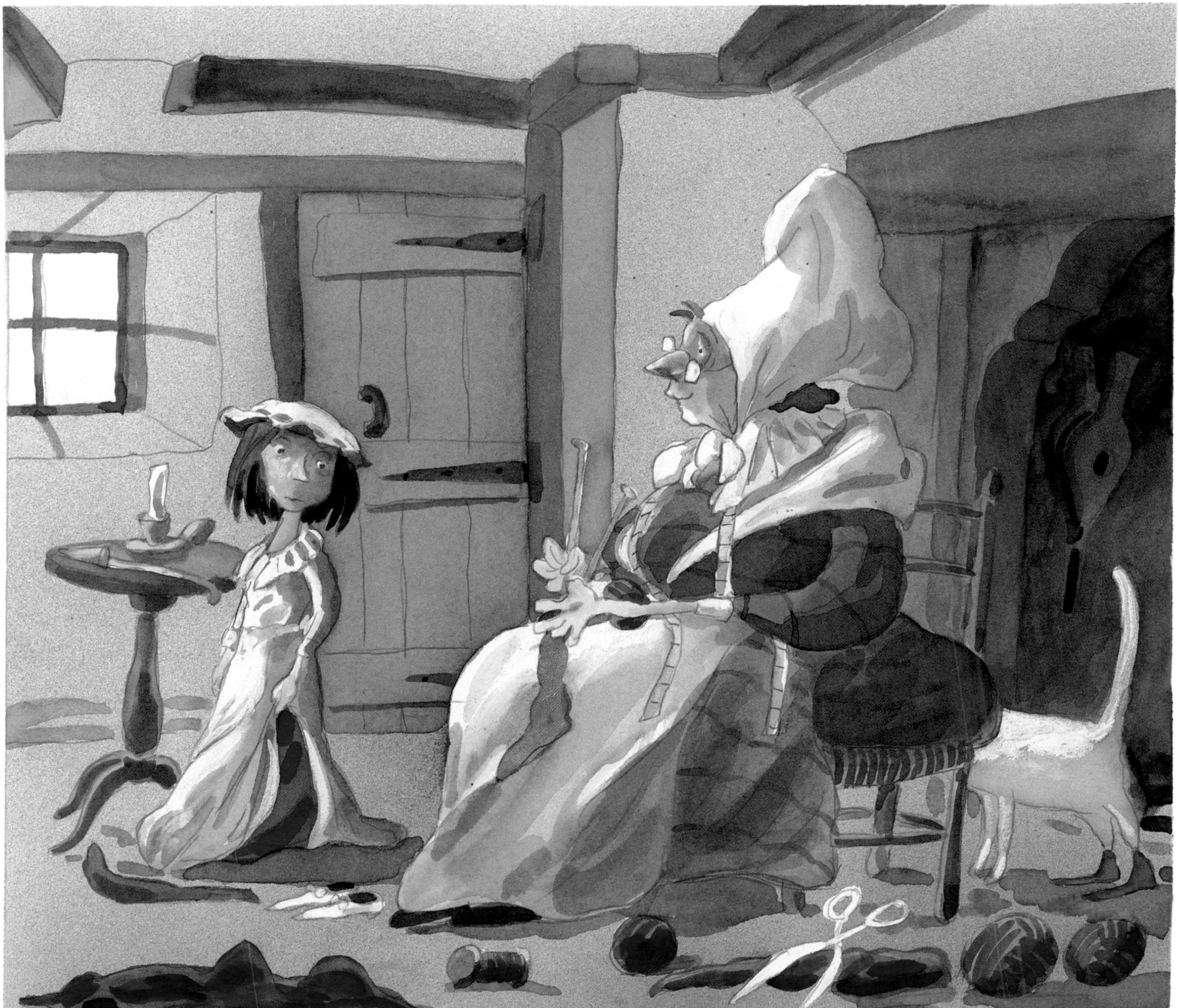

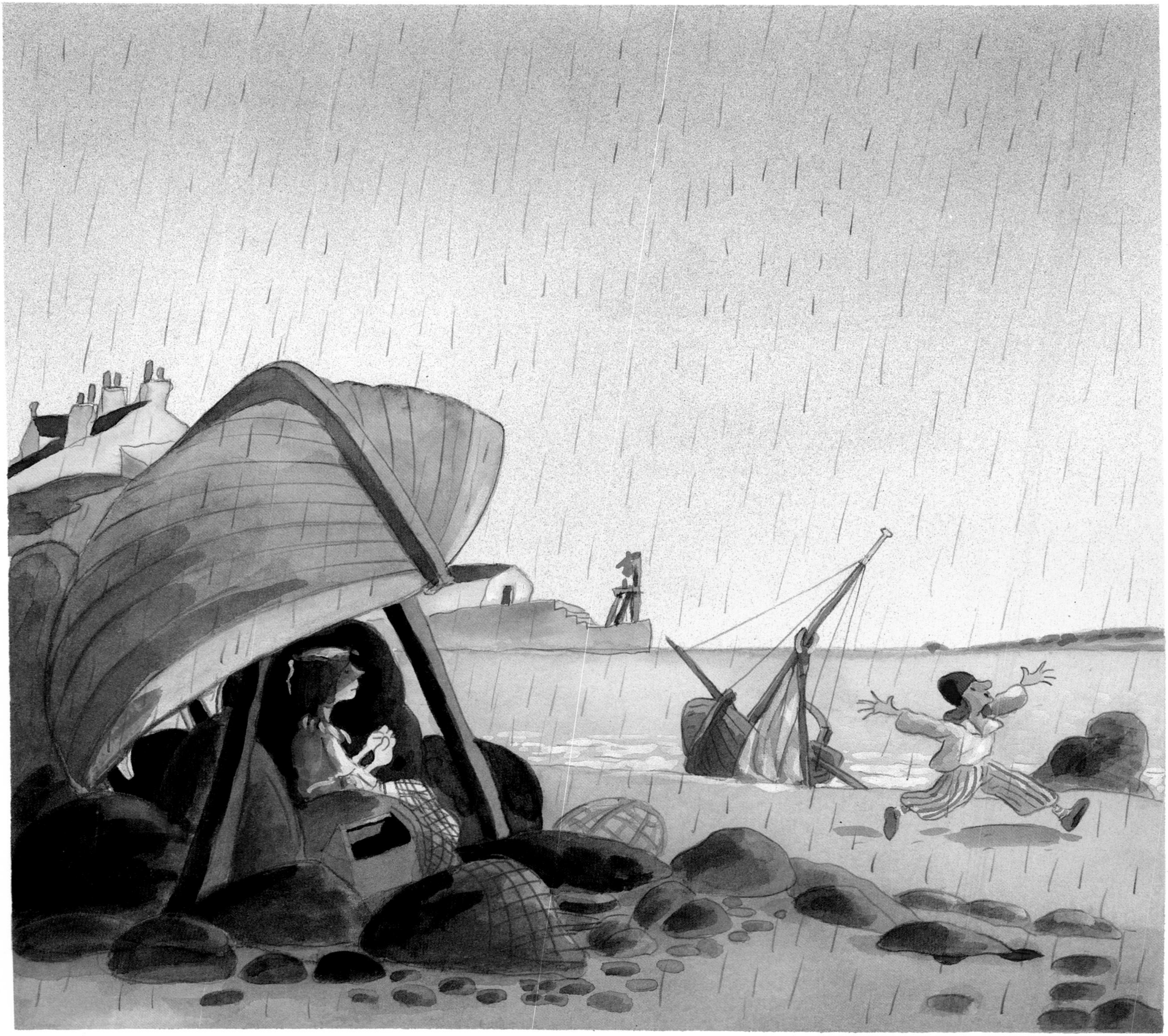

ONE RAINY morning, Trewenna was sitting under an upturned boat, mending nets, when she heard a splash and a crash, and there was her dad, beaching his boat in a great hurry, and running up the shore.

"Sound the alarm!" he cried. "Call up Lord Talbot! Old Bonaparte is at Sennen Cove with three French warships, their guns loaded, and ready to land!"

Trewenna was first to the alarm bell, pulling at the rope, her hands all cold from the nets and slippy with fish scales.

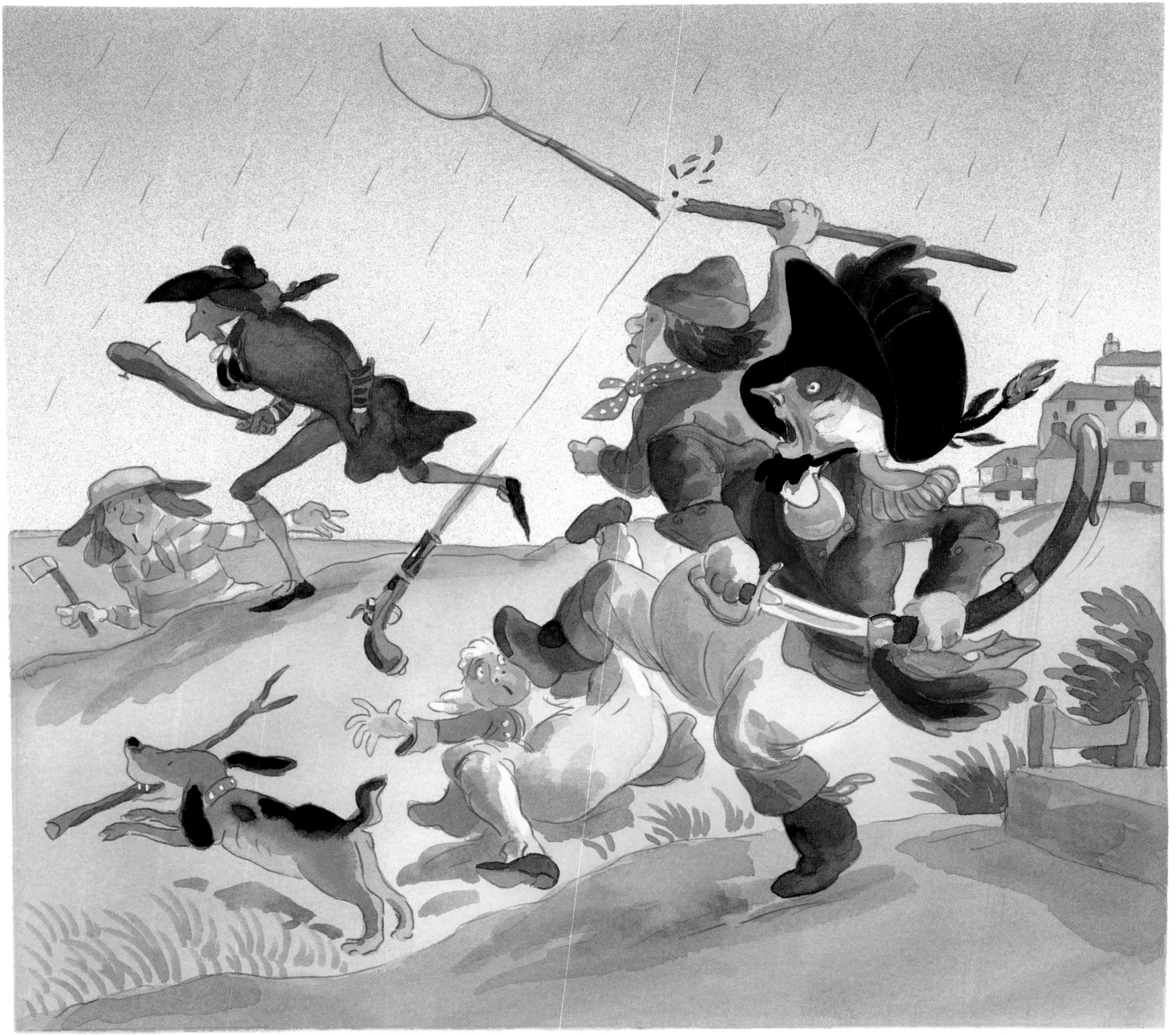

DOORS flew open up and down the village street, and from his big house up on the hill, Lord Talbot ran, waving his sword and calling for his horse.

"Hey! Hector!"

"Neighhh!"

The fishermen caught up any weapon they could find. An axe, a spade, a pick, the poacher's rusty musket and two old flintlock pistols.

"Goodbye, my hearts," said Trewenna's dad, catching up Trewenna and her gran, and giving them both a smacking kiss.

"You'll be safe and sound here. Lord Talbot is calling for the redcoat soldiers to protect you, and we'll send Old Boney packing, to be sure."

And he was away up the hill with the other men, marching behind Lord Talbot, on their way to Sennen Cove.

IT WAS quiet in the village.

The women stood anxiously together, waiting for the redcoats to come marching down the street, with their high black boots and shiny guns, to protect them from Old Boney.

The rain cleared, a dog barked, the waves slapped the quayside, but still the redcoats didn't come.

"Don't fidget so, Trewenna," said her gran.

"I'll just watch from the wall," said Trewenna, and she slipped away quickly, before her gran could argue.

She ran along the cobblestones, right to the end of the sea wall.

First she looked landward. Then she looked seaward. And then she saw a warship, sailing quietly up behind the headland.

No one could see it but Trewenna.

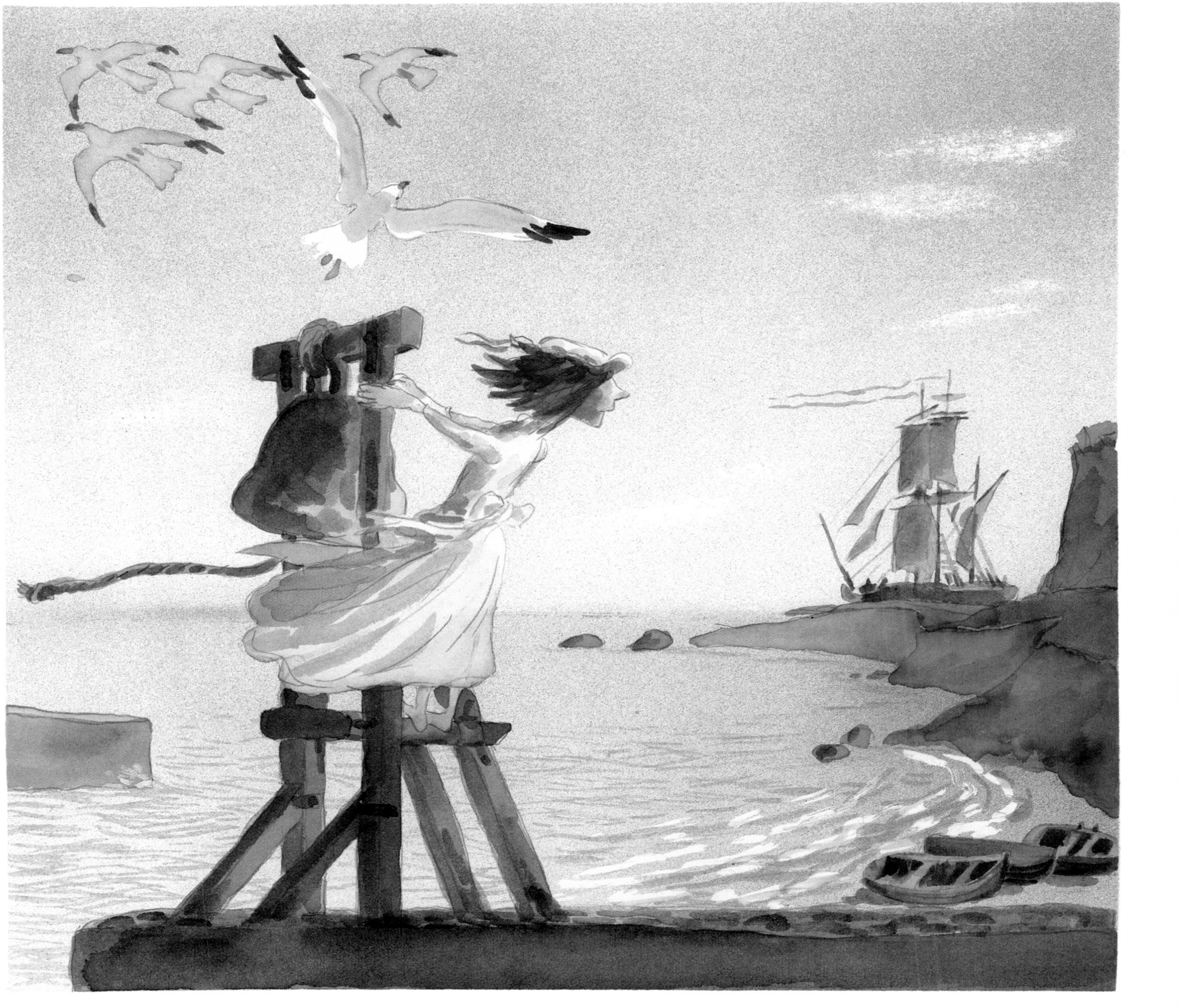

FIRST ONE, then two, then three French warships came sailing, their flags streaming in the wind, their decks lined with silent French soldiers holding guns and swords, all ready to come secretly ashore and take the village by surprise.

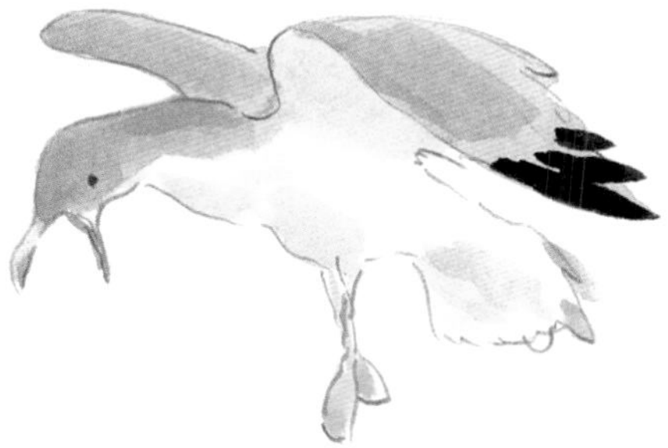

Trewenna ducked down behind the wall. She darted back to the village, faster than a herring, faster than a mackerel.

She shrieked like a seagull,
"Old Boney is coming! Old Boney is coming!"

Snatching up their babies, catching up their shawls and bonnets, shouting for their children, the women began to run.

They clattered up the village street towards the cliffs, to the dips and hollows among the gorse bushes where they could hide from Old Boney and his soldiers.

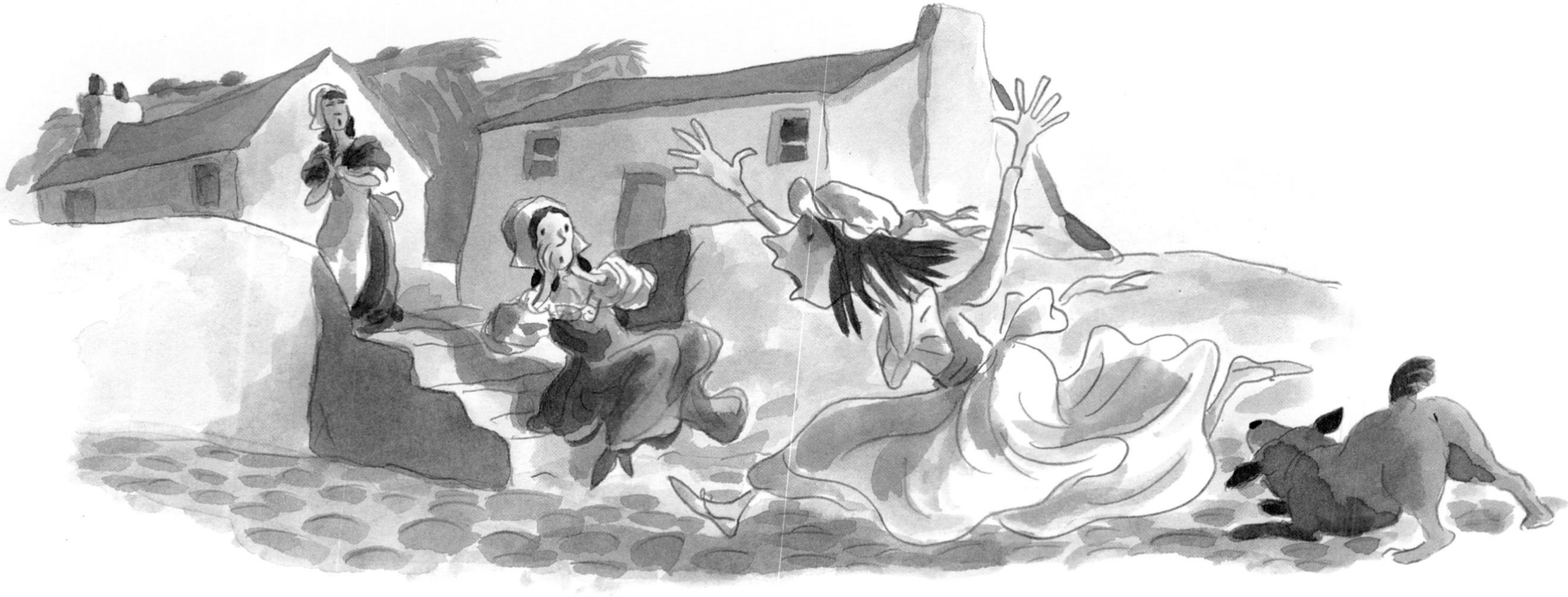

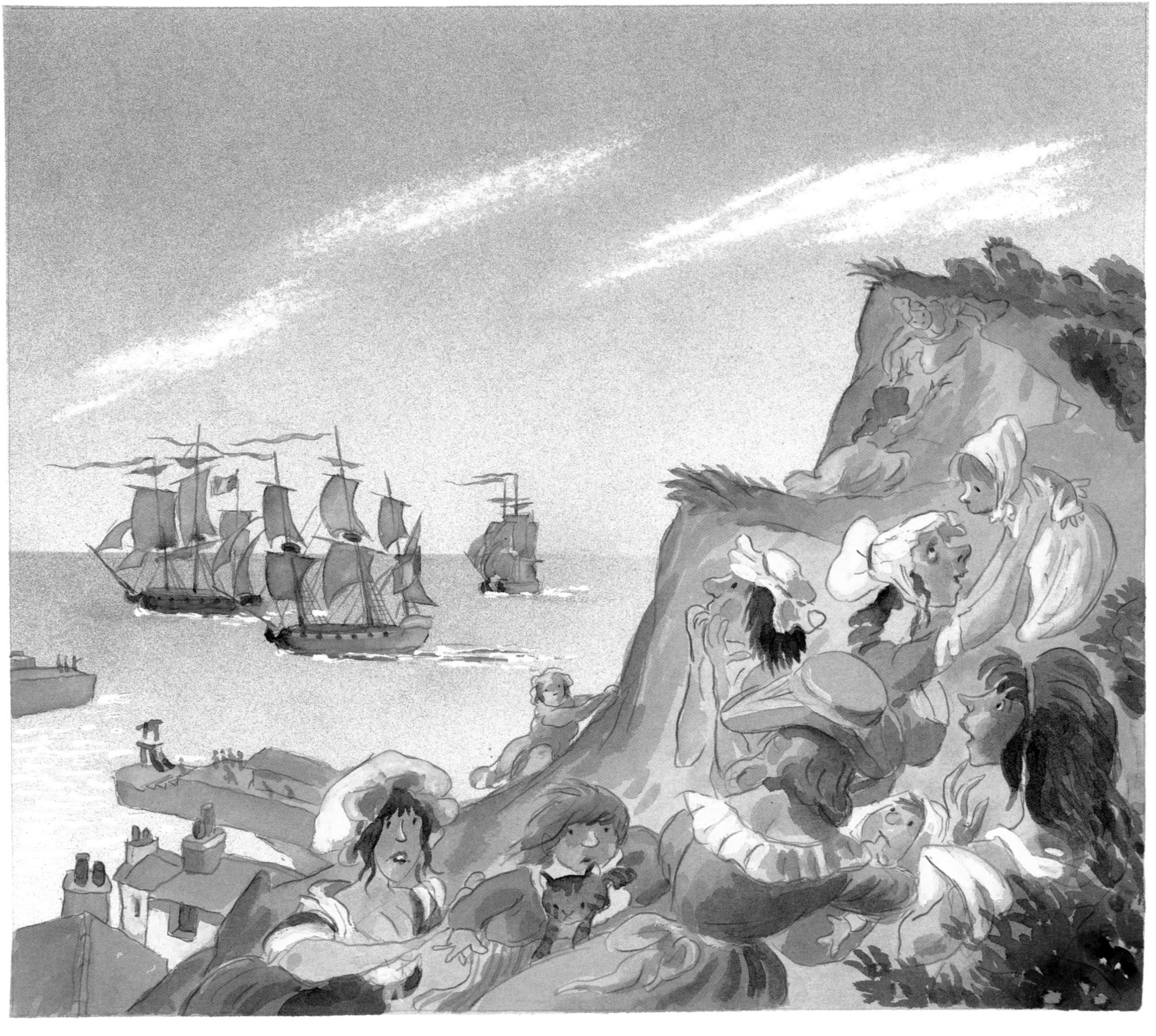

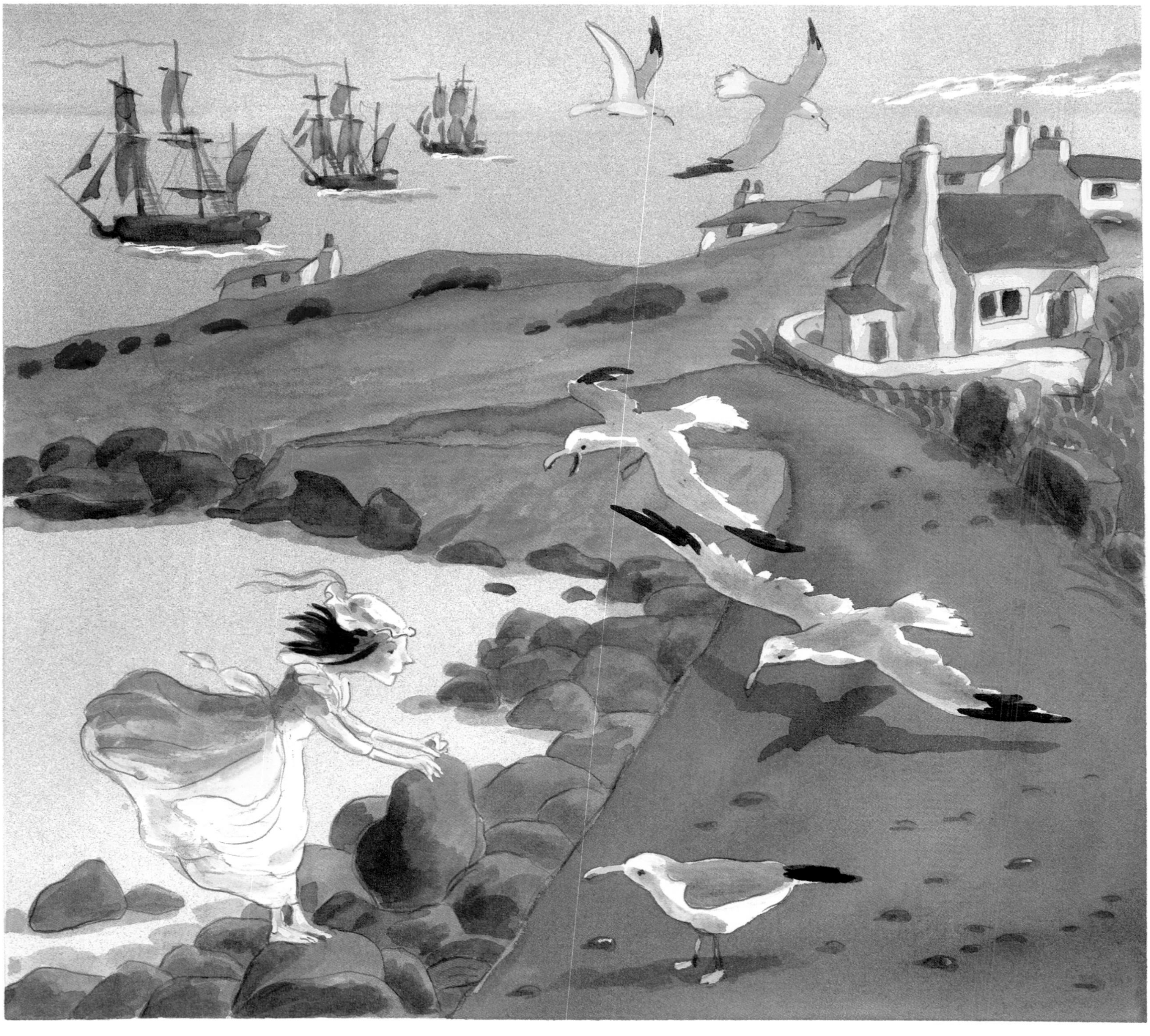

BUT Trewenna's gran caught her arm.

"Wait!" she panted. "Where are your socks, Trewenna? Where is your red flannel petticoat?"

"Oh GRAN!" cried Trewenna. "What does that matter NOW?"

"You never can tell," said her gran.

So Trewenna ran back to get her socks and petticoat.

When she lifted the stone, there they lay, as red as cocks' combs, as red as holly berries, as red as a robin's breast . . . as red as the jackets of redcoat soldiers.

Trewenna stood and looked at the red socks and petticoat, and an idea came into her head – a crazy, mad idea.

She bundled them under her arm and raced up the cliff track, zigzag, like a rabbit, among the gorse bushes.

UP THERE on the clifftop the women crouched, hiding with their children.

They could smell the heavy, almond scent of gorse flowers.

They could hear the plosh, plosh, plosh as boatloads of soldiers were lowered from the warships.

They could hear splash, splash, splash as the soldiers began to row steadily to shore.

They could see the glitter of swords and muskets, and the pale faces of the soldiers as they looked up at the cliff, to make sure no redcoats were waiting for them there.

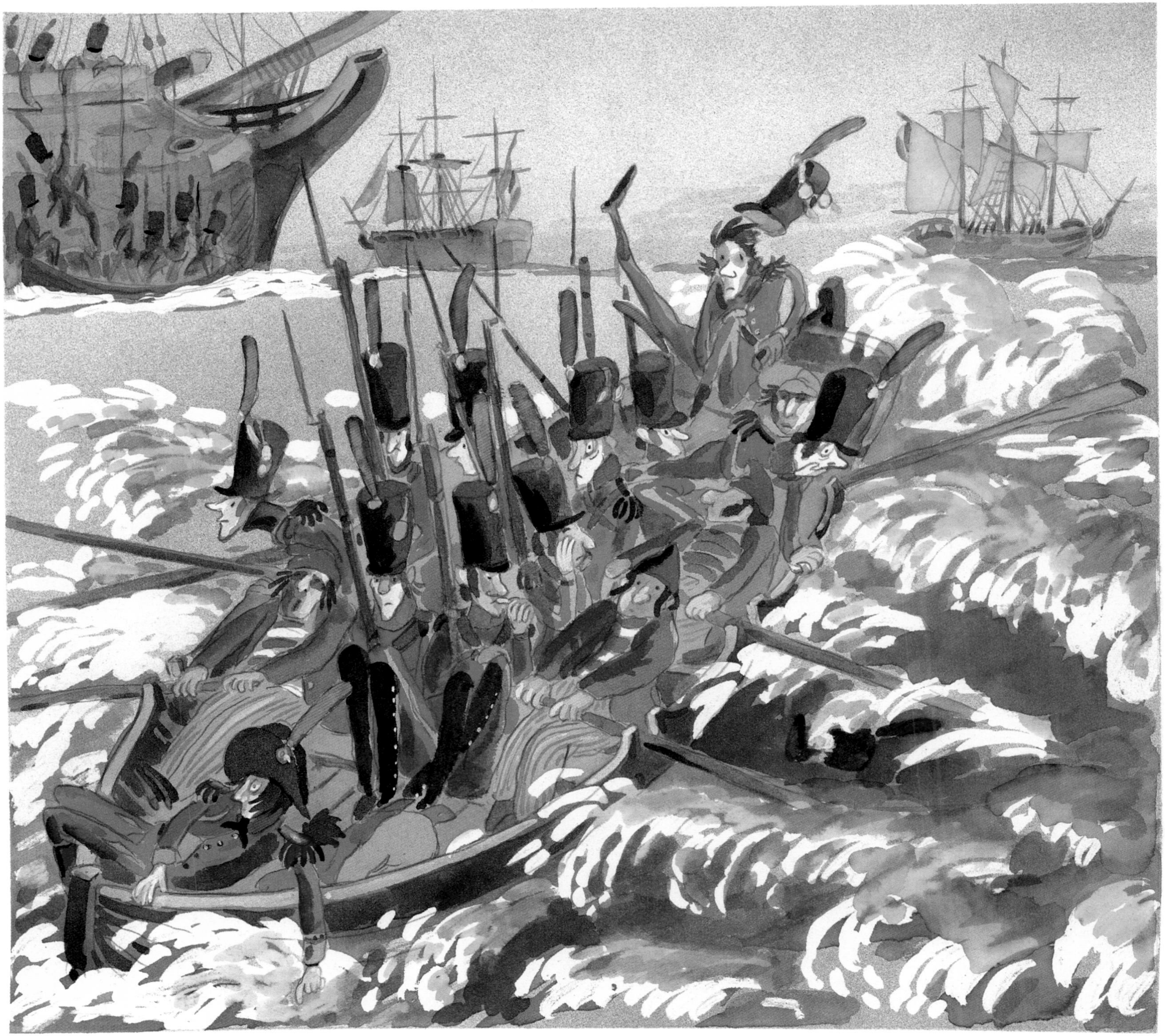

THROUGH the bushes, slipping silent as a weasel, came Trewenna, with her bundle of petticoat and socks.

"Gran," she panted.

"Hush, my sweeting. Not a sound," breathed her gran.

Trewenna put her lips to her gran's ear and whispered something.

"It's crazy! It's mad!" exclaimed her gran. But she began to smile. "Go on then," she said.

Trewenna crawled under the gorse bushes from one woman to the next, her knees pricking, her hands stuck with gorse pins, giving them the message.

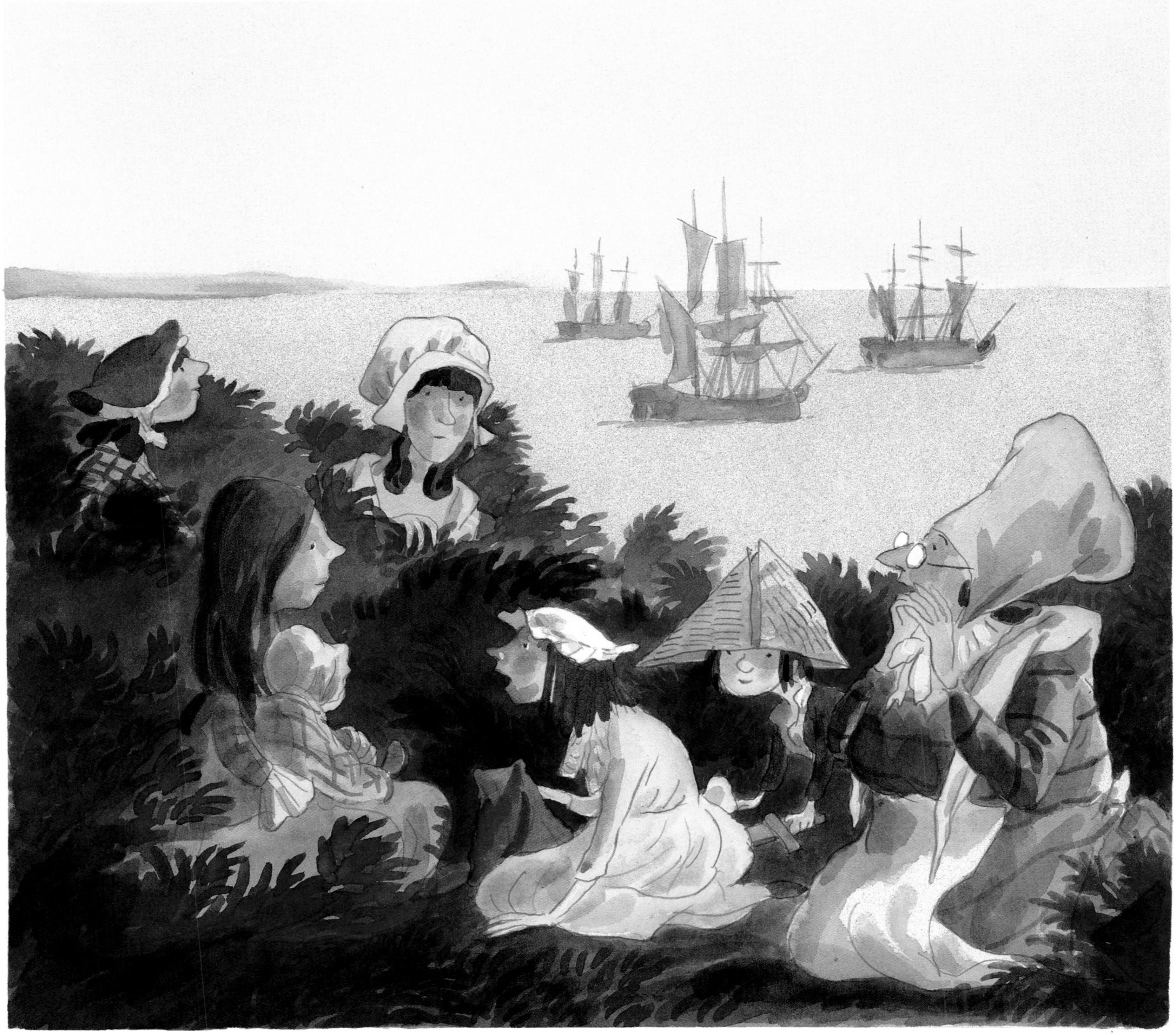

DOWN on the seashore Old Boney's soldiers leaped from their boats onto the wet sand. They were smiling to see how easy it was to trick the Cornish fishermen. They were laughing to find no redcoats there to stop them. They began to march together up the sandy beach towards the village. One, two! One, two!

Click, clack! A stone came rattling down the cliff path.

The soldiers faltered. They looked up among the rocks and bushes. They saw a flash of red. Then another, then another. The more they looked, the more they saw. All along the clifftop they caught glimpses and flutters of red, coming and going, half hidden in the gorse.

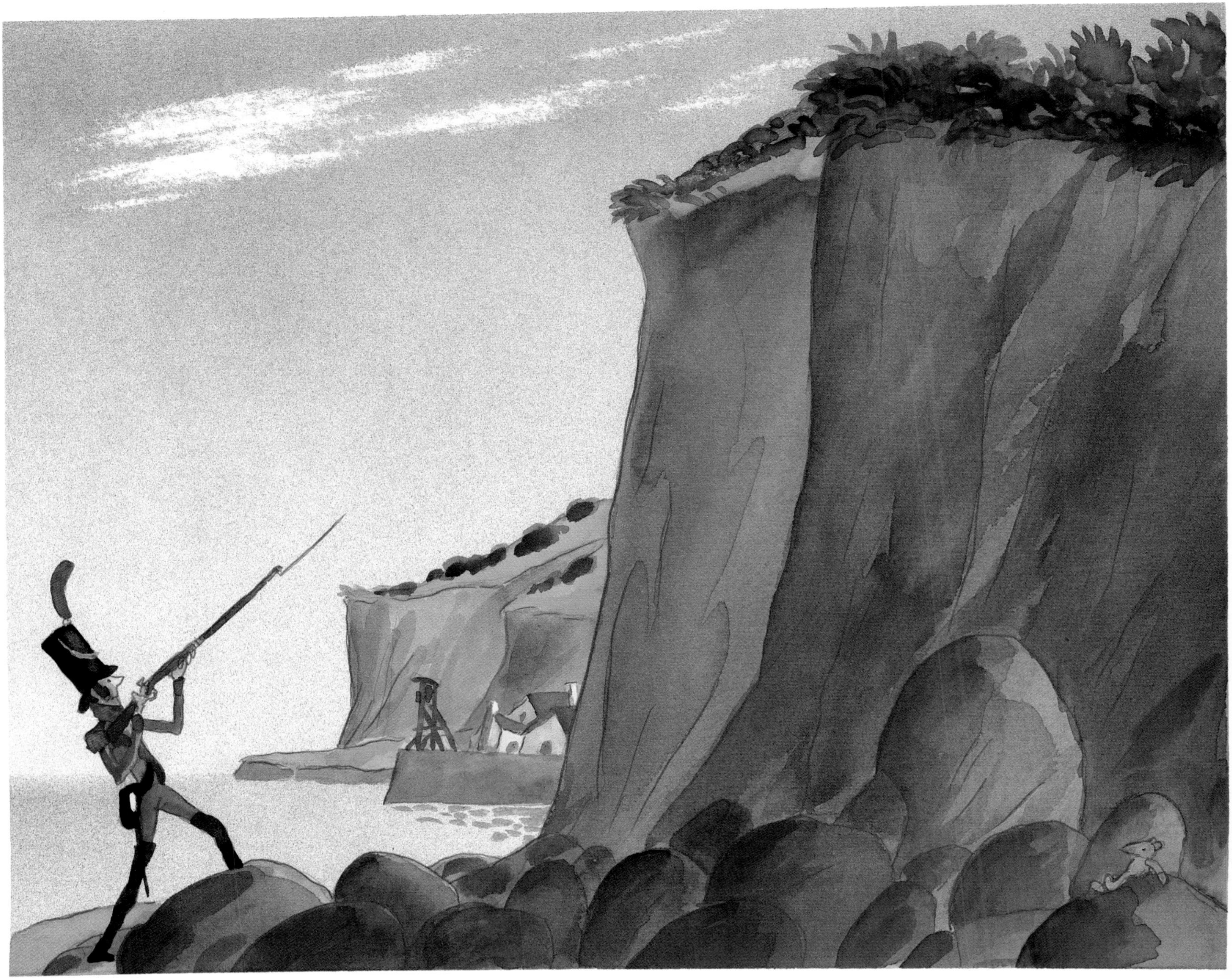

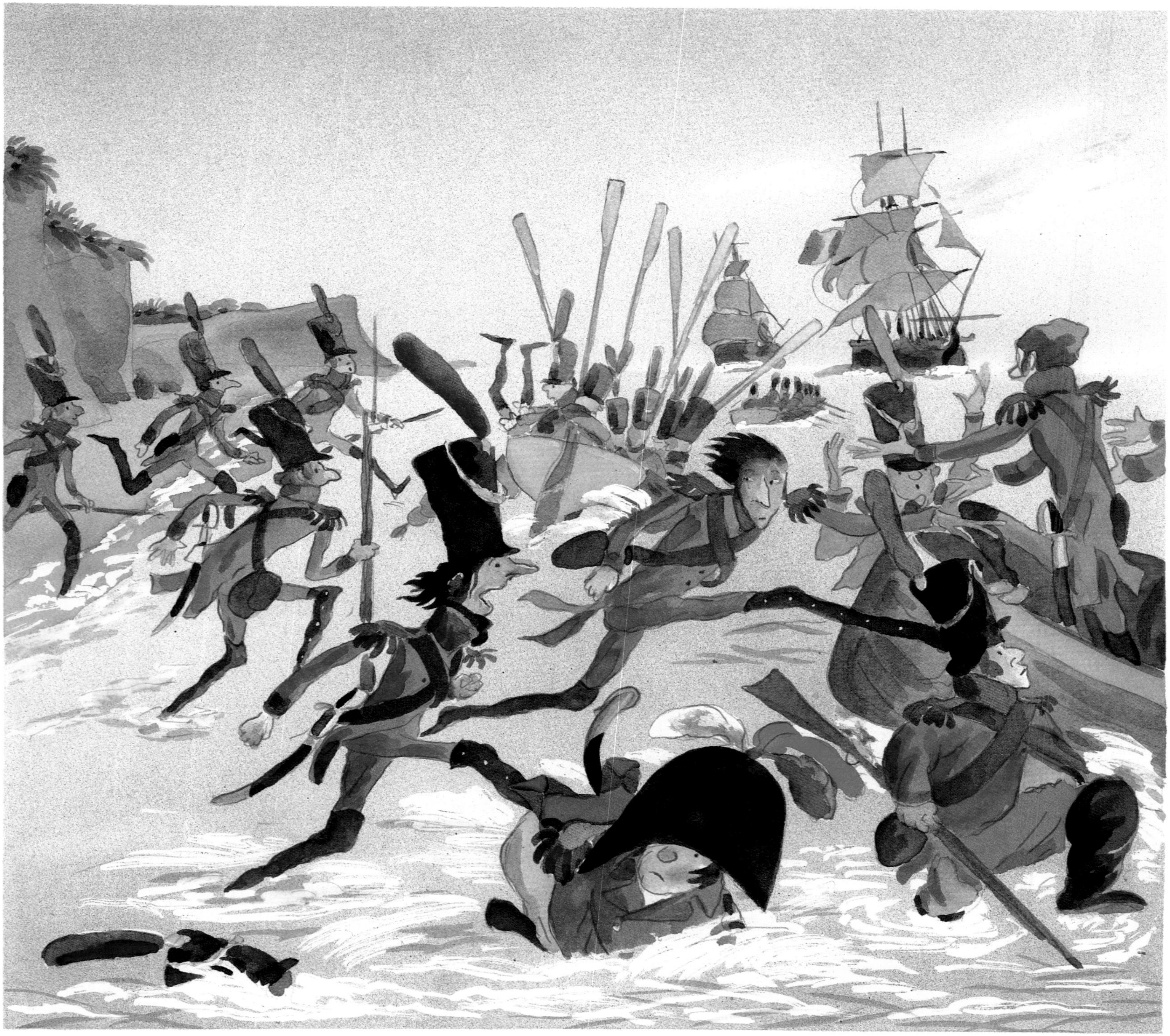

"AMBUSH!" shouted the soldiers in front, turning upon the soldiers behind. "It's the redcoats!"

"AMBUSH! AMBUSH!" came the cry, as the soldiers behind turned in fright and stumbled back towards the sea.

"An army of redcoats! Hundreds of redcoats! Ready to attack!" yelled the soldiers.

How they hurled themselves back into their boats! How they slipped and swore! Out at sea the great warships were waiting for them, their sails set, all ready to escape from the fierce redcoats on the Cornish cliffs.

Old Boney was on the poop deck.

"A narrow squeak," he cried. "Back to France, my men. Back to France!"

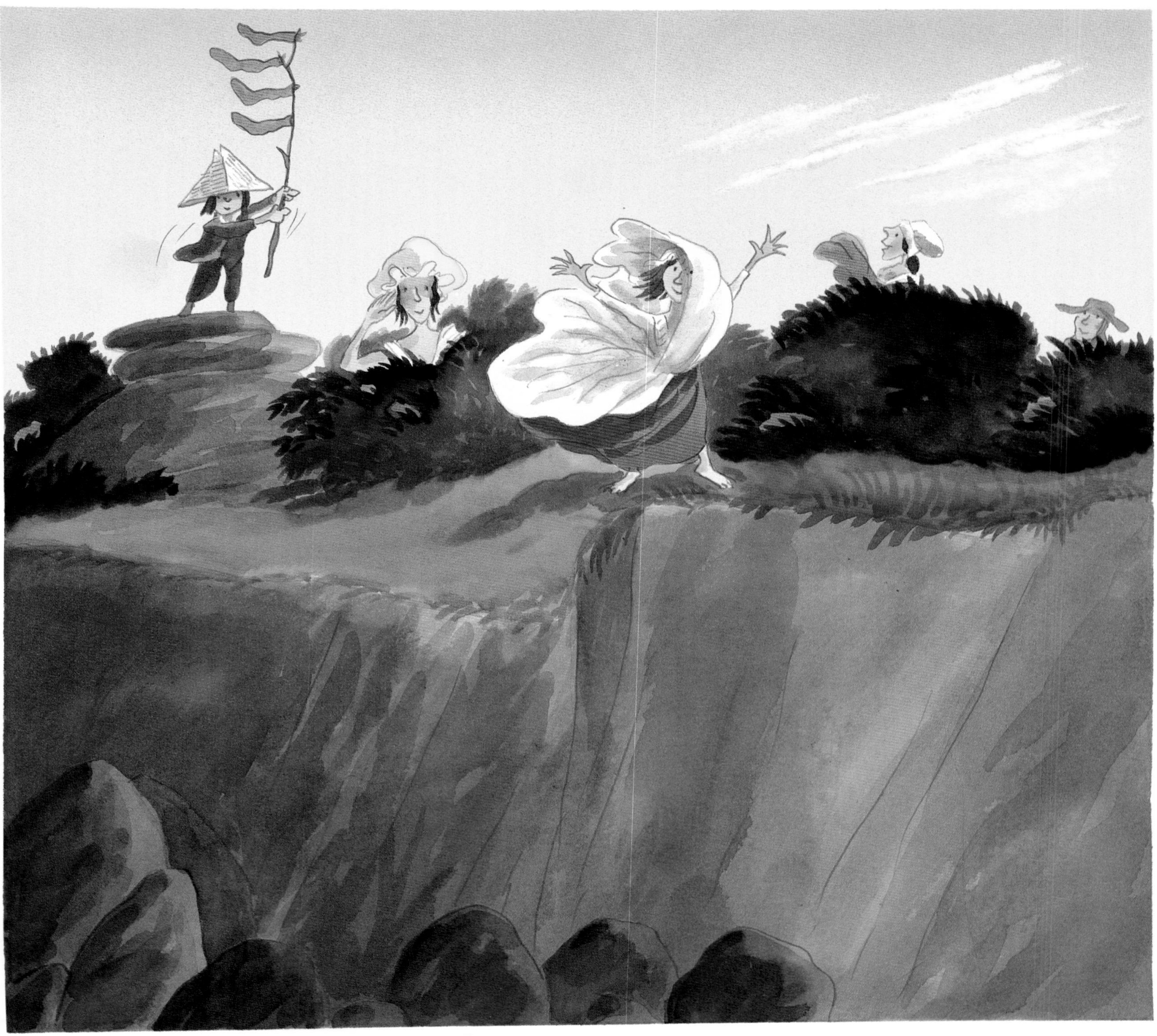

TREWENNA stepped out from behind a gorse bush. Her skirt was over her head, and her red flannel petticoat was blowing in the breeze. She pulled down her skirt and looked out to sea. The French warships were sailing over the horizon. She looked across the clifftop. Far and near, red flannel petticoats fluttered and flew among the bushes.

Anyone would think a whole army of redcoats was hiding there, just waiting for Old Boney himself.

"ALL CLEAR!" shouted Trewenna.

The village men came marching home that evening with Lord Talbot at their head. They were tired and hungry.

From every cottage came the smell of baking pasties, and on every doorstep sat the mothers and daughters of the village, sewing up long rents and tears in their red flannel petticoats.

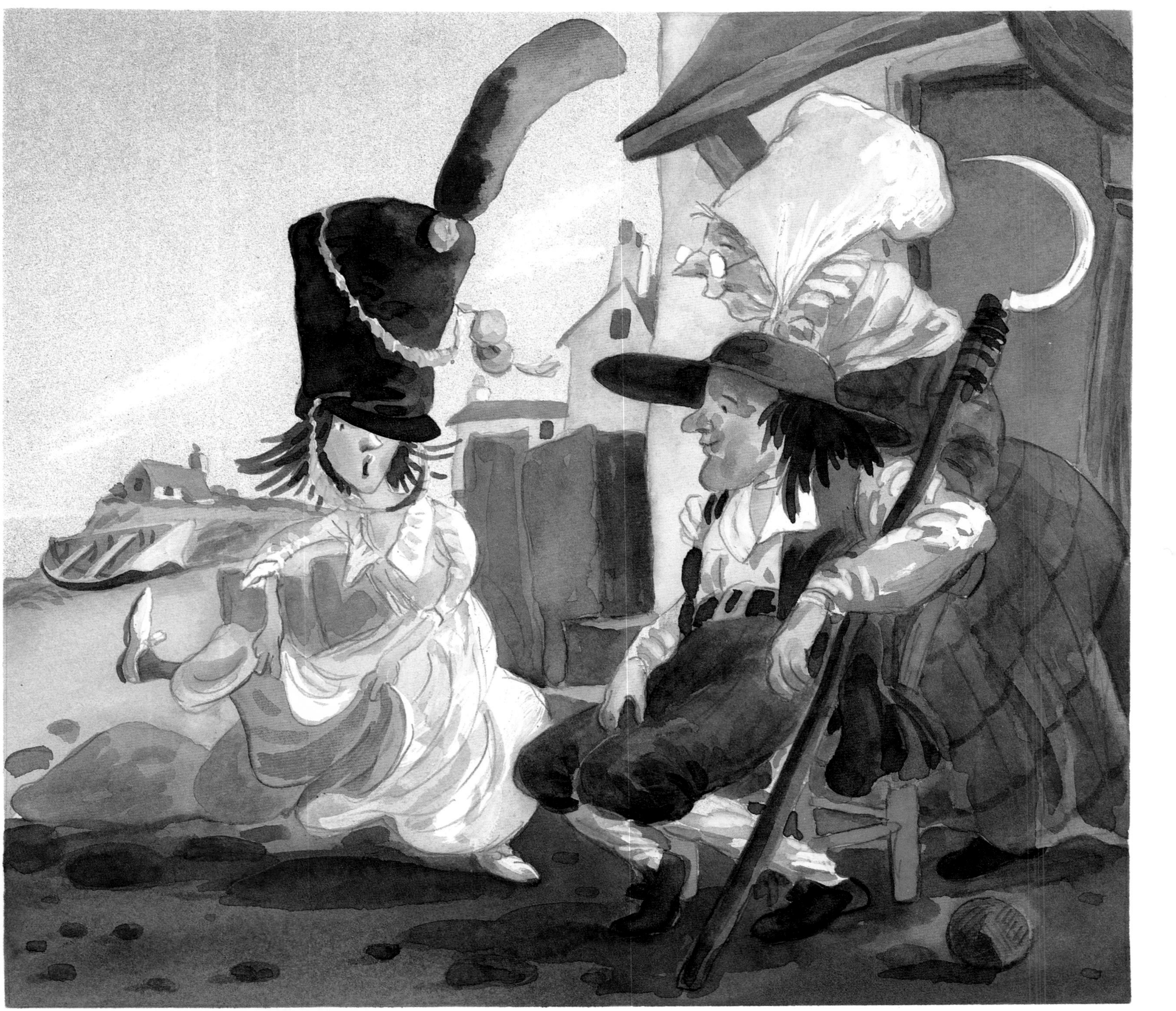

TREWENNA'S dad sat down heavily beside Trewenna and her gran.

"Well, my dears, we searched every bay from Sennen to Zennor, and not a glimpse did we get of Old Boney and his men."

"We did though," said Trewenna, busy threading her needle.

"WHAT!" cried her dad, starting to his feet. "And did the redcoats come? And was there a battle?"

"No, no Dad," said Trewenna calmly.
"We didn't need the redcoats at all.
We just flapped our petticoats at
Old Boney and he sailed back
to France."

"You never can tell when a
red flannel petticoat will come
in handy," said her gran, and
she went indoors to fetch the
hot pasties for supper.